The Castle of Ladies

The Castle of Ladies

Retold by Constance Hieatt

Illustrated by Norman Laliberté

Thomas Y. Crowell Company/New York

THE CASTLE OF LADIES
THE JOY OF THE COURT
THE KNIGHT OF THE CART
THE KNIGHT OF THE LION
SIR GAWAIN AND THE GREEN KNIGHT
THE SWORD AND THE GRAIL

Library of Congress Cataloging in Publication Data
Hieatt, Constance B.
The Castle of Ladies.

A story of Sir Gawain and the Castle of Ladies based on certain episodes in the grail ro-
mances of Chrétien de Troyes and Wolfram von Eschenbach.
[1. Knights and knighthood] I. Laliberté, Norman, illus. II. Chrestien de Troyes, 12th cent.
Perceval le Gallois. III. Wolfram von Eschenbach, 12th cent. Parzival. IV. Title.
PZ8.1.H534Cas   398.2'2   75-187945
ISBN 0-690-18064-0

Designed by JILL SCHWARTZ

Manufactured in the United States of America
ISBN 0-690-18064-0
1 2 3 4 5 6 7 8 9 10

For Adam

Contents

Preface   ix

1 SIR KAY'S QUEST   1

2 TOURNAMENT AT TINTAGEL   9

3 A GAME OF CHESS   19

4 AN UNGRATEFUL KNIGHT   29

5 CROSSING THE LAST RIVER   37

6 THE PERILOUS BED   47

7 THE SWORD OF THE STRANGE SCABBARD   55

8 SIR GAWAIN'S QUEST   65

Preface

The core of my story of Sir Gawain and the Castle of Ladies is to be found in certain episodes in the grail romances of Chrétien de Troyes, who wrote in the twelfth century, and Wolfram von Eschenbach, of the early thirteenth. In the works of Chrétien and Wolfram, the Gawain episodes form a subplot, in counterpoint, but clearly subordinated, to the main plot; Sir Gawain himself is a courtly foil to the hero Perceval (or Parzival). It would seem, nevertheless, quite likely that the story of Gawain's adventures at the mysterious Castle of Ladies had some prior independent existence, from which the later poets borrowed it to turn it to other purposes in the story of the quest of the grail. What the original shape of the tale was—if, indeed, it did exist—there is no good clue to tell us. But similar enchanted castles, and similar challenging ladies, quite often seem to have a connection with the ambiguous reputation of Morgan le Fay.

And so I have chosen to put Morgan at the heart of the mystery here, and to establish some logical connections between this episode and those which precede and follow it. In so doing, I have fused the Proud Lady of Logres with her near relatives in Malory (Books VII and IX), and developed motifs from mere hints: the Sword of the Strange Scabbard, for example, was suggested by Chrétien's "Espee as Etranges Renges," mentioned in passing at a crucial point by the grail messenger, but never ex-

ix

plained or used later in his unfinished romance. Other source materials included the medieval bestiaries, which inform us of the fascinating traits of such creatures as the basilisk; the allegorical *Romance of the Rose;* and even Spenser's *Faerie Queene.* These and other ingredients should be familiar to fellow devotees of Arthurian literature, but the brew is my own.

Although much of the shape of the story thus originates with me, lovers of the tradition may be assured that I did not invent the characters, not even King Arthur's dog. I hope that readers of *Sir Gawain and the Green Knight* will not be puzzled to find Morgan le Fay, old and ugly there, now young and beautiful: these guises are part of Morgan's famous sorcery. They will certainly find Gawain's courtesy familiar, sorely tried though it is in this adventure where the very model of chivalry is a victim of mistaken identity at every turn and must endure some unusual insults and rebuffs. For here is no unproved youth, striving to earn a reputation for prowess, but the knight to whom all others must be compared, coping with a series of highly embarrassing situations in which his name and reputation are unknown.

The Castle of Ladies

Sir Kay's Quest

When all the world was young and Arthur was king of Britain, there was no merrier place anywhere than the court at Camelot. There one could see the noblest knights and ladies in the land, dancing and playing games like carefree children; the sound of laughter and sweet music was heard from morning to night there. Frowns, tears, or voices raised in anger were rare in those gracious halls and gardens. But there were times when things went wrong, as they do everywhere. This late spring day was, unfortunately, one of them.

A strange silence seemed to have descended on Camelot. Few people were to be seen; those that were about moved very quietly, keeping their voices low, for the king was in a fretful mood and none dared to disturb him. Even his queen, Guinevere, had withdrawn with her ladies to her private quarters, leaving King Arthur to himself—except for one young page, who sat in a corner of the room, piping a faint and mournful tune on his flute. The king did not seem to notice the subdued music as he paced about the chamber, or stood peering glumly through the casement window.

It was thus that his nephew Sir Gawain found him, tapping a finger upon the window sill and staring out into the distance. "My dear lord," said Sir Gawain, "be of better cheer! The sun is shining, and the hedges are fragrant with roses. Will you not come out and walk in the garden? Even the dogs are anxious for your company—see, Caval lies in the doorway, with his head between his paws, hoping that you will join him."

King Arthur sighed. "Perhaps he, too, knows that all is not well in this household. Perhaps he is even hungry, for since my good steward, Sir Kay, left on a quest last month, all is mismanaged and neglected here."

"Say not so, good sire," protested Gawain. "The servants are doing their best to please you, and provide all that is needful for horses and hounds, as well as for men and women."

"But nothing is done the way it is when Sir Kay is here," the king complained. "The kennels and stables and kitchens are all in need of direction."

"Then I shall direct them for you myself, lord," Gawain replied. "I shall start at once with a look at the kitchen."

For the first time in days, King Arthur began to laugh. "What, good nephew," he said, "can you order provisions for us, and help the cook oversee his staff? I do not think you are used to the company of bakers and dairy maids, and I fear you know far more about swords and lances than you do of roasting spits!"

"Nay, lord," said Sir Gawain. "When I was a boy in my father's land of Orkney, there was not a room in the castle where I was not at home. I have helped to turn many a spit, and pulled many loaves from the oven."

"Then, if it pleases you," the king said with a smile, "go to the cook, and see that he has planned dishes fit for the knights and ladies of Camelot."

"I shall do better than that," said Gawain. "Tonight I shall watch over every step in preparing and serving the supper. I vow

that you will say Sir Kay himself could not manage a more splendid feast."

"Well said, nephew," Arthur replied. "For my part, I shall go and see how the horses and dogs are faring."

And so it was that when evening came, and the court gathered at the tables in the great hall, Sir Gawain was not seated at the high table in his usual place of honor by the side of the queen. Tonight he was in the kitchen, for he wished to be quite sure that every roast was done to a turn, every sauce seasoned perfectly, and every pastry brought to the table with fanfare and decorum. Sir Lucan, who had charge over the king's cellars, saw that the very best wine was brought out, and the court was merrier than it had been for many a day—especially when, in the middle of the meal, Sir Gawain himself came out of the kitchen, dressed in a cook's smock and carrying a roast peacock on a great silver tray.

King Arthur laughed until the tears rolled down his cheeks to see his nephew, the most famous knight of his court, leading a solemn parade of serving men bearing meat; but Gawain's expression did not change. With great solemnity, he knelt before his king and presented the splendid dish, while all the court applauded.

At just this moment, a confused clattering sound was heard in the courtyard, and the doors suddenly swung open. Into the hall marched two gnarled dwarves, bowing under the weight of a litter, on which lay, very still, a knight covered to the chin by his cloak. Behind the litter walked a tall and handsome lady bearing a shield. Everyone knew the arms on that shield at once: it was Sir Kay's, and the knight borne on the litter was Kay himself.

The knights and ladies of Camelot were frozen with horror to see that motionless figure, and for several moments no one spoke

4

or moved; then the lady stepped forward and placed Kay's shield before the king. She laughed, not very pleasantly. Her dark eyes flashed, and she tossed her gleaming black hair as she glanced about the court, then finally turned back to address Arthur, in his high seat.

"Have no fear for your precious Sir Kay, king," she said rather rudely. "He is not dead, and will live to make a fool of himself again, I have no doubt. He can neither speak nor move right now, but in good time his tongue will be as sour as ever, and he will regain his strength—such as it is, though he seems a useless wretch at best. And this is what passes for help from the most famous court in the world!"

"Fair lady," said King Arthur, "we thank you for bringing Kay back to us, though we grieve to see him so silent and helpless. But what can have happened to him, and who are you who speak so scornfully?"

"Lord," said the scornful damsel, "I am called Maudisante, lady of Logres. Some weeks ago, I sent one of these my dwarves to your court to ask your help most urgently. As my messenger then told you, my sister, the lady of Montesclaire, has been taken captive by a wicked enchanter. He has cast her into a foul prison, where she is guarded night and day by a fearsome monster. No man, no matter how brave he may be, can pass that terrible guardian and free my miserable sister, unless he can first arm himself with the Sword of the Strange Scabbard. With that sword, and only that sword, the beast may be slain. Sir Kay knew this when he undertook the quest. But alas the day when you sent me such help as his! I guided him, and taught him how he could win the Sword of the Strange Scabbard, but he could not hold his foul tongue nor control his temper long enough to gain the right to use the weapon.

"Without it, he had no chance against the beast that guards the dungeon. Yet he would not listen to reason, and insisted on attempting the rescue—doomed to failure from the start. Now he is paying the price of his folly, and it will take all the skill of your physicians to bring him back to his feet before the summer is over. For shame, O king, that you would send this clown on such an errand! He would have perished himself if I had not rescued the would-be rescuer."

"For that, we are indeed grateful, dear lady," said the king. "But be assured that we shall not forsake your sister; if need be, my whole court shall ride to save her."

The damsel Maudisante sniffed scornfully. "I have no need of an army," she said. "I ask only one good knight, of strength and courage and wisdom. But if yon Sir Kay is a fair example of your court, I fear I shall not find him here!"

Sir Gawain now took a step forward. "Lady," he said, "accept my aid. I shall go wherever you say, and do your bidding in every way, to rescue your captive sister."

"Merciful heaven!" cried the lady, putting up a hand to stop him from approaching nearer. "Have I come all this way to be so insulted? A greasy kitchen boy, no less! Are there no true knights in this court?"

"Lady," said the king, "there is no truer knight in the world than the man who offers you his help. Indeed, he is—"

But the lady would not hear him, and could hardly contain her fury. Stamping her foot, she cried, "Alas, that ever the day should come when the most famous court of the world has nothing to offer a maiden in need but a fool and a dirty, wretched kitchen boy! Alas for Britain, for its days of glory are surely past when Camelot can come to this!"

Wringing her hands, she gestured to her dwarves to come with her, and was about to leave the room, when Arthur rose in his place and said, "Give ear, damsel, for God's love. How can we send you help if you do not tell us where to go? I swear you shall have such aid as can give you no cause to lament."

"I put little faith in your words," said she. "But if any good knight can be found, tell him to come to my land of Logres, far in the west. If such a one does not come within a fortnight, I fear it will be too late, for my poor sister cannot last much longer; she has endured too much torment already."

Then she mounted her horse and rode on her way, with no company but the two dwarves. Gawain could not go with her, for he was unarmed, and hardly dressed to ride out; but he left the hall at once, calling for his horse and his arms.

7

Tournament

at Tintagel

It was not long before Sir Gawain, fully armed, took a hasty leave of the king and queen and rode off on his good horse Gringolet. King Arthur begged him to wait until morning before starting his journey, but Gawain would not hear of it. And so he rode throughout the night, and on through the morning, hardly stopping for rest at all. Around noon, he came out of a forest and through a narrow valley, at the end of which he saw a plain where many banners waved in the sun. Gawain pulled Gringolet's reins short, and proceeded very carefully, for it looked rather as if there were a great army camped on the plain. Sir Gawain would never have fled from a battle, like a coward; yet he had no wish to be delayed on his quest.

As he approached the field, he saw tents pitched all around the edge; Gawain therefore dismounted, so that no one would think his intentions hostile, and led his horse as he passed the camp. Soon he met a squire, who was leading a horse from the large town which, Gawain now saw, was just beyond. The squire stopped and greeted him courteously. "Sir," said the squire, "if you intend to take that horse to the tournament, you have missed your turning—you should have taken the path to the right back there."

Sir Gawain was relieved to hear that it was a tournament, and not a war. He thanked the squire, but told him that he had no intention of going to a tournament. "Tell me, though," he added, "who is holding the tournament, and what this city is."

"This is Tintagel, good sir," said the squire; "and if you wish for glory as a knight, you must surely mount your horse and ride to the great tournament our lord, Count Tibaut, is holding today. The count has sworn that the winner shall have his daughter in marriage. The lady is one of the loveliest maidens alive, and he who wins her hand will some day rule Tintagel, for our lord has no son."

"I think I have heard of the maiden," said Sir Gawain. "Is she not called Obille?"

"That is her name," the squire replied.

"But I have also heard," said Gawain, "that she was promised to the young lord Meliance de Lys. Was not his father a dear friend of Count Tibaut?"

"That is quite so," said the squire. "We had always heard that the two young people were devoted to each other, and that one day they would marry. But it is said that Obille has refused the love and service of Meliance, vowing that she will not have him unless he proves himself as a knight and wins her from all others. That is why the tournament is being held: Obille wishes to marry the best of the knights that compete for her favor, and Meliance wishes to prove himself that knight. But he will not be unchallenged! Come, sir, and try your prowess on the field, or you are no true knight."

His words troubled Sir Gawain sorely, for never had he turned his back when there were challenges to face. But his quest might be in peril if he were to allow a delay, and he knew he must ride on with all haste to the land of Logres if he were to come to the aid of the lady of Montesclaire. And so he excused himself, much to the surprise of the squire, and went on toward Tintagel, still leading Gringolet by the bridle.

But Gawain and Gringolet had been traveling now for many, many hours, and both of them were weary. So, when Sir Gawain reached the walls of the city, he tethered the horse and sat down to rest a while, before he went on to seek for some food and drink. As he rested there, he became aware of voices from the ramparts above his head. The countess of Tintagel had come out, with many other ladies, to view the knights riding to the tournament. You may be sure that the fair Obille was among the most eager of the ladies to see every detail, but her younger sister, Obilot, who was a child not much more than eight years old, was every bit as excited.

As the ladies caught sight of Gawain, sitting under an olive tree, the countess asked, "Who is that knight below? Can you see his shield?"

Obille replied, "That is no knight, Mother. He has come away from the field, and is clearly not going to the tournament. He must be a squire or a servant, carrying his master's shield—unless he is a merchant, which may well be the case. Perhaps the horse is for sale."

"That cannot be so," said the little girl, Obilot. "He is most certainly noble and brave. See how handsome he is! Oh, how I wish he would be *my* knight! How pleased I would be to reward him for his service—"

"The service of a low fellow like that is exactly what you deserve, you silly baby," said her sister angrily. "I tell you, he is a merchant."

"I do not think you know a good knight when you see one," retorted Obilot. "Did you not spurn the faithful love of Meliance de Lys? Yet, good knight as he is, Meliance would be no match for *my* knight, I am sure."

"Cease your childish nonsense," cried Obille. "Do not talk of Meliance, or I shall give you a sound beating. *Your* knight, indeed! Who would be fool enough to serve an infant like you?"

The countess now tried to stop her daughters' quarrel, but little Obilot ran off, laughing at her sister's anger. Whispering in a corner to her playmate, whose name was Claudette, she said, "Obille thinks that all the knights will ride for *her* today, though she secretly hopes that Meliance de Lys will win her in the tournament. But I should like to show her that she is not the only lady for whom a knight may compete! Come, let us ask the knight who rests below to joust for my sake today."

"But how could we reward him?" asked Claudette. "We have nothing to give him but our toys."

"Oh, we will think of something," Obilot said. "But come now, hurry, before he goes away."

And indeed Gawain was preparing to leave the spot, much embarrassed by the conversation he had overheard. The two little maidens ran swiftly down the hill to the gate of the town and caught up with him before he had moved many paces.

"Pray stay, sir knight," cried Obilot, "and hear a maiden's plea. Surely, as a true knight, you will not refuse me."

"Little lady," said Sir Gawain, "heaven forbid that I should be discourteous, but I have vowed to help another, and I may not tarry here."

"Say not so," said Obilot, "for I am as worthy to be served as any grown-up lady. My father is a count, and I will reward you with my love. I shall not be like some ladies, who think they are too fine to love the knights who serve them."

"Surely your love will be a precious gift, fair maid," said Sir Gawain, much surprised—never had he been asked to serve so tiny a lady before! "I cannot think I deserve it."

"You shall earn it," said Obilot, "if you will only ride in the tournament for my sake. It will not delay you long, for the jousting is about to start. Wear my sleeve as a token, and be my knight, I beseech you." With these words, Obilot pulled the sleeve from her right arm, and tied it to Gawain's lance.

Sir Gawain gazed down on the little girl, who now stood there with one bare arm, smiling hopefully up at him. *Well,* he thought, *it is a knight's duty to serve those who ask for his help, and some good may come of it; to refuse would certainly be discourteous.* And so Gawain mounted his horse, and grasped the lance, from which flew, like a banner, a very small sleeve indeed. "Maid of the Little Sleeves," he said, "I shall do your bidding. Mind that you remember to reward me with your love."

"Oh, I shall," cried Obilot, clapping her hands with joy, as her knight rode off to the tournament.

Now the trumpets sounded, and the drums beat, and the stands were crowded with ladies in their brightest dresses as the knights rode onto the field. More than a hundred noble knights were there that day, but none seemed more likely to take the prize than the splendid young knight Meliance de Lys, who rode on a great bay charger. He was a dazzling figure with the sun glinting from his golden helmet. As he rode past the stands, and the crowd gave him a mighty cheer, Sir Meliance turned to bow to his beloved Obille, who cast down her eyes and would not favor him with a smile—

but she hoped, in her heart, that he would be the day's victor.—
That is, none seemed more likely than Meliance, except for the
tall stranger who rode with the little sleeve on his lance. As the
tournament went on, the knight of the little sleeve seemed to be
everywhere at once, and always victorious in every meeting, as he
swept rider after rider into the dust. At last the time came when all
others had been forced to retire from the field, and Meliance was
left to face his unknown opponent in single combat. The crowd

held its breath—and each of the count's two daughters prayed that her special favorite would win.

Now Sir Gawain proceeded with caution, holding back from using his full strength, for he knew how badly Meliance wanted to win the day's prize, and had no wish to deprive him of his lady. Meliance used all his skill, but he was not, of course, really a match for such as Gawain. Had he known whom he was riding against, he would have laid down his arms at once! But he did not, and he attacked boldly, while Sir Gawain parried every thrust and gave every appearance of giving him a sharp battle. And so it went on, until the sun was about to set and the count called a halt to the duel.

The lady Obille wept bitterly as the two knights obeyed the count's command and turned their horses toward the stands. She feared that Meliance would, after all, fail to win the promised reward, and she was all the more shamed when the strange knight removed his helm and she recognized the man she had dismissed as a merchant and a low fellow. But Obilot's joy was unbounded when her knight stepped forward and said, "My lord count, give your daughter to Sir Meliance, who has fairly won the prize you offered. For I did not fight for the lady Obille, but for yonder Maid of the Little Sleeves: her love is the only reward I ask." He pulled the now-tattered sleeve from his lance, and, with a bow, returned it to the young maiden.

And so, in the end, the count joined the hands of Obille and Meliance, to everyone's great pleasure—not least, that of the lady herself! He then turned to his younger daughter, and said, "Obilot, you too have had a fine knight fighting for your favor. Can you tell us who he is?"

"He will have to tell you that himself," said the little maiden, for of course she did not know his name.

"I am called Gawain," said that knight, "son of King Lot and nephew of Arthur of Britain."

"You are heartily welcome to Tintagel, Sir Gawain," said Count Tibaut, overjoyed to have so famous a guest. "Pray accept our hospitality tonight—and, indeed, for as long as you care to honor us."

Much as Gawain longed to be on his way, the hour was late, and he was very tired and hungry, so he consented to stay for that night. There everyone crowded about to do him service, and to bring him the choicest of food and wine. The count asked him to take a place of honor at the table, between the countess and the lady Obille, but Gawain preferred to sit with Obilot—who proudly wore the sleeve that had seen so much action that day— and her playmate, Claudette. Count Tibaut urged him over and over to stay for the wedding celebrations, which would begin the next day, but Gawain explained that he was riding on a quest of grave importance, and that he must be off before dawn the next morning.

"Oh, take me with you," said Obilot.

"Alas, sweet little lady, I fear I cannot do that," said Sir Gawain. "I fear your mother, the countess, cannot spare you to me."

"Then must we say farewell? I pray that you will return one day, to claim the love I owe you," said the maiden with a sigh. "I have little else to give you as a reward for your faithful service. Unless you will accept this from me, the only treasure I have—a golden ball. Will you take it? Perhaps it will bring you luck."

She held out the ball to him. It was somewhat larger than an orange, and very pretty. Sir Gawain accepted it gravely, as he kissed her goodnight and took his leave. He did not know it then, but the time was to come when he would owe his life to Obilot's ball.

A Game of Chess

ong before anyone else in the castle was stirring in the morning, Gawain had saddled Gringolet and ridden off toward the west. All that day he rode on through fields and forests, passing villages and fording streams, but avoiding the towns and castles. Evening fell when he was in a great swamp, with little firm ground or shelter; but man and horse made the best of it, and rested on a grassy hummock during the night. In the morning they came upon a spring of fresh water, where Gawain found a drink to go with the bread and cheese he had brought from Tintagel. Then he rode again on his way. For several more days he made his way through wild and desolate country, until an afternoon when he met a young lord hunting in the woods, with many huntsmen, horses, hawks, and hounds.

By this time, Gawain felt sore need of a good meal and a night under a roof, so he turned his horse into the lord's path, greeted him with all courtesy, and asked whether there were a town or castle nearby. "Indeed, sir," said the young knight, "my own castle of Cavalon is less than an hour's ride, if you follow the path beyond the left bank of the stream. Sir, do not think me discourteous if I do not ride back with you now; my men are eager to go on with the hunt, and I do not wish to turn back yet. But my fair sister, the lady Belacuel, is at the castle. She will make you heartily welcome, I assure you, for my sake. I will send my page along with a message for her, if you will excuse me from coming myself."

"My dear sir," said Sir Gawain, "I have no wish to spoil your sport, and will gladly find my way by myself."

"That will not be necessary," said the lord of Cavalon. "My page will show you the way. I shall return in the evening, then, and look forward to your company. In the meantime, I am sure that my sister will treat you just as she does myself."

The two knights bowed to each other, and the hunting party rode off, while Gawain, led by a young page, turned in the direction of the castle.

Soon they entered a walled town where the streets were full of people. Merchants displayed their wares in canopied booths, and money changers were to be found on every corner. Blacksmiths and armorers were busy at work; the town seemed full to bursting with skilled workmen. Gawain saw many rich shields and fine swords displayed as the page led him through the bustling crowd toward a fair castle that stood in a park beyond the marketplace.

They rode straight into the courtyard, before the great hall of the castle, where servants came running, relieved Sir Gawain of his armor, and led away the horses to the stables while the page took the knight into the presence of the fair Belacuel. There, before the lady, the page knelt down and delivered his lord's message: "My lady," said he, "my lord your brother bids you to receive this his guest as if he were your own brother, and to treat him with all kindness."

The lady turned a gentle and smiling face toward Sir Gawain. She was lovely, with sky-blue eyes and soft hair the color of red gold curling gently around her rosy face, as she held out dimpled white hands to greet the knight. "Sir," she said, "you are truly welcome to Cavalon." And she held up her face to be kissed.

Gawain gave her a kiss in greeting. Then he found her welcome so pleasant he kissed her again.

Now Belacuel led Sir Gawain to a seat beside her own, and signaled to the servants, who quickly brought cakes, and fruit, and wine which the maiden offered to Gawain with her own dainty hands. And there they sat, and talked, and laughed merrily together in all comfort and joy, until the lady asked Gawain if he would care for a game of chess. He agreed gladly, and a splendid chess-

board was taken down from a hook on the wall and placed before them.

The game proceeded slowly for a while, but soon the knight was winning, and the lady frowned in concentration as she tried to decide what move to make next. "Nay, fair one," said Sir Gawain; "do not mar your forehead so—you look much more lovely when you smile." And he reached over and took her hand.

Belacuel glanced up at him through long eyelashes, and did not pull her hand away. He thought perhaps it was time for another kiss, and leaned forward over the table to reach her lips. But just then a white-haired knight ran in through the doorway, and froze to a halt. Pointing an accusing finger at the chess players, he cried, "What are you doing, my lady, to behave so brazenly with this our enemy? Vile knight, take your hands off our mistress—Is it not enough that you have tried to attack our lord and steal our treasure once, but you also sneak back here like a false traitor when the lord is away?"

He set up a great cry, and called the men of the household and the townsmen in the streets to take up arms and defend the castle, while Gawain and the fair lady drew back in alarm.

"Alas, lady," said Sir Gawain, "how shall I defend myself, without my sword and shield?"

"Quick," said the lady, "let us take this chess set and flee into that tower there!" Sweeping the pieces together, she fled up a flight of stairs, with Gawain right after her—and just in time, for a horde of angry, shouting men were pouring into the room.

While the armed men of the castle tried to force their way into the tower room, a mob of townsmen collected in the street outside, trying to scale the wall in order to storm the tower itself. Gawain looked about in desperation for a weapon to help him hold back

his assailants, and found only a bolt that had once been used to fasten the tower door. The maiden passed him the chessboard, which had a ring on the back from which it had been hanging on the wall; with this for a shield, brandishing the iron bolt as his only weapon, Gawain held back the human tide at the door.

24

Meanwhile the resourceful lady took up a position by the window, where she took aim at those who were trying to make their way up and pelted them with chessmen—knights and rooks and bishops became deadly missiles in her hands, for this was no ordinary chess set, but a fine one with large, heavy pieces.

At the height of the fray, the young lord of Cavalon came riding back into the town, and was stunned with astonishment to see the raging battle. "Halt!" he cried in a terrible voice. "What are you great fools doing, attacking my sister and my guest? Put up your weapons at once!"

The crowd wavered, and fell back. But the white-haired knight who had started all the trouble stepped forward and said, "My good lord, do not be so hasty. This is the same villainous knight who attacked you yourself not long ago and attempted to steal the castle treasure! I recognized him by the curious design in the silk from which his horse's trappings are made. It is the same!"

"Is this true, sir knight?" the young lord asked sternly.

"I do not know what you mean at all," Gawain answered. "I have never been here before in my life, nor laid eyes on you, to the best of my knowledge. It is true that my horse is decked with silk of a strange design, but so are almost all the horses from the stables of King Arthur.

"I fear you have mistaken me for some other knight of Arthur's court, sir," he added, turning to the white-haired knight.

"I do not believe you," said that knight, though he seemed a bit doubtful now. "I think you are Sir Kay, returned to attack us again."

Now Gawain began to understand something of what must have happened. He informed them courteously that he was not Sir Kay but Sir Gawain, and told them how Kay had been brought back from his quest looking more dead than alive. At last they saw that he was telling the truth, and they ushered him back into the great hall with many apologies.

It was not until after a fine dinner had been served, and the wine passed to everyone's satisfaction, that the young lord of Cavalon asked his guest what his errand might be in that distant part of the world. When Gawain had told him of Kay's failure in the quest to free the lady of Montesclaire, and of how he himself now rode on that quest, the lord smiled and said, "Now it is clear to me why Sir Kay acted as he did. But he was most foolish and rash. You see, the Sword of the Strange Scabbard is the greatest treasure of our family, and we would never give it into any man's hands except for grave cause. The need of the lady of Montesclaire would have seemed cause enough; but Sir Kay did not tell us about that. Rather, he demanded the sword, and, when I refused to hand it over to him at once, tried to take it by force. My men here saved me from his attack and drove him from our land. Perhaps you will now forgive them, sir, for their behavior toward you: Sir Kay's treatment of us was hardly courteous."

Sir Gawain blushed for his comrade's folly and ill manners, and assured the lord that there was nothing to be forgiven. "But," he added, "is there any hope that you will let me take the Sword of the Strange Scabbard? Without it, it seems certain that my quest will fail, and an innocent lady will perish in misery."

"Alas, sir," answered his host, "I fear that it is too late. After Sir Kay's rude attack, we feared for the safety of our treasure, and sent it, for safekeeping, to the mistress of the Castle of Ladies."

"I have not heard of the Castle of Ladies," said Sir Gawain. "But perhaps you can tell me the way thither, so that I may beg its mistress to let me have the use of the sword?"

"The way is not very hard to find," said the lord, "but I fear you will never come within, where the sword is now kept. That is why we thought it would be safe there. No man has ever penetrated into the Castle of Ladies, and it is much to be doubted that any man ever will."

"I can but try," said Sir Gawain.

"Then I shall wish you luck, and you will need a great deal of it," said the lord of Cavalon. "In the morning, I will show you the road which leads through the land of Logres; beyond it, on the edge of the sea, stands the Castle of Ladies."

Gawain was, at least, glad to hear that he would come to Logres first, for he was anxious to find the scornful damsel Maudisante, and to show her that he intended to free her suffering sister if it could possibly be done.

An Ungrateful Knight

When Gawain left the next morning, the lord of Cavalon and his sister rode to the edge of the forest with him, to send him on his way, and a great troop of knights and serving men escorted them with great ceremony—the very same men who the day before had so suddenly attacked the tower where Gawain and the lady had gone to seek for safety. Now Sir Gawain parted from them in all friendliness, and once again the lord expressed his sorrow at the treament Gawain had met at his castle. The sweet lady Belacuel wept a little, sad to see her guest depart; Gawain bade her a tender farewell, kissing her once more before he rode into the woods.

For some time, he saw no living creature but the wild beasts of the woodland, who fled from the path at the sound of Gringolet's hoofs. He heard no voice but those of the birds, singing high in the treetops. Then, when the noonday sun could be seen directly above in the sky, Sir Gawain found himself entering a large clearing, where the grass whispered in the breeze. There he saw something gleaming and flashing in the sunlight, and, when he looked more closely, he saw that it was a shield, with a spear, propped against the trunk of a tree. Not far away, he now noticed, a horse was standing—but a more wretched and broken-down wreck of a horse one could hardly imagine. It was not that it was old, but it had evidently been in terrible battles, or met with some fearful abuse, for it was lean and trembling, and hung its head dejectedly. Wondering who could have brought weapons here with such a horse, Gawain dismounted and looked further.

The tree against which the shield and spear leaned was a great oak, with a trunk so thick that it completely hid the figure that lay behind it from Sir Gawain's sight. Now, as he rounded the tree, he saw a knight lying so motionless upon the grass that at first

30

Gawain did not think that he could be alive. But he knelt down and gently removed the knight's helmet and loosened his armor; he could find no sign of a wound. He looked at the silent, ashen face, and picked up the knight's wrist, thinking to cross his hands upon his breast; but, to his surprise, he felt a pulse beating faintly in the wrist, or so it seemed. Thoughtfully he laid down the clammy hand, and looked about for a bird's feather. When he found one, he placed it on the man's lips and watched. It seemed to stir gently every few seconds. The knight was not dead, he decided, but wounded in some strange fashion, or severely ill.

Now Sir Gawain was wise in the lore of plants, and he knew how to use healing herbs to treat the sick and wounded; however, there was nothing but meadow grass to be found in this glade, so he resolved to go on and find help, and then to return. There was little he could do now for the knight, except to cover him with his cloak and see that he lay in a position that might be comfortable.

The dejected horse took no notice of all this. It did not even turn its dull eyes to watch Gawain ride off on Gringolet.

Soon Gawain found the trees thinning out. He saw that he was entering a fertile plain, filled with vineyards and orchards. Ahead of him, the road slanted up and ran spiraling around a steep hill, toward the shining towers of Logres. The castle was perfectly round; at first glance, it looked as if it were a top spinning on the summit of the hill. All around the hill grew a hedge of wonderful fruit trees, bearing figs and nuts and pomegranates, and throwing their shade over delightful garden walks.

As Gawain drew closer, he saw a spring bubbling up in the shade of an olive tree, and he turned to get water for himself and his horse. A lady in a rich brocaded gown sat on a rock by the spring. Her raven hair was tied up with golden bands, and bright

31

jewels gleamed on her fingers, for this was the lady of Logres, the damsel Maudisante. Gawain was very happy to see her. He dismounted from his horse at once, giving the lady a fair greeting.

But the damsel did not return his courtesy. Her dark eyes blazed with fury, and she drew back her silken skirts, shrinking away from him. "So!" she said in an angry tone. "It is King Arthur's kitchen boy. Did I not tell you that this was no business for the likes of you? Get out of my sight, before you earn the disgrace you so richly deserve!"

"Be patient, good lady," said Sir Gawain; "I shall do my best to prove that I am worth more than you think."

"Ugh," said the lady with a sniff: "you smell of grease and onions!"—of course, this was not true, but Gawain could hardly argue the point—"And does your master, the cook," she continued, "know that you have run off on this fool's errand?"

"I come with the approval of King Arthur and all his court," Sir Gawain replied. "As I came on my way here, I learned tidings of the Sword of the Strange Scabbard. It is in the keeping of the mistress of the Castle of Ladies; if you will show me the way thither, I will do my best to win it."

The damsel burst out laughing. "What!" she said. "*You* propose to do what no man has ever done before, and enter the Castle of Ladies to beg a sword from its mistress? I can hardly wait to see your face when you see what lies in store for you there! Well, then, if you are so determined to play the hero, I will consent to ride with you. It can do no good for my poor sister—I fear that her cause is hopeless! But, at least, it may be afford me some amusement. If you wish to go on with this, turn into the meadow, over the bridge through that orchard there, and fetch my horse for me."

Sir Gawain promptly did as he was told, and soon led back the lady's horse. He wished to help her mount, but she would not suffer him to touch her, and preferred to climb into her saddle un-aided. As she was gathering up her reins, he spoke again, saying, "Wait a while yet, fair lady, for there is something I must do before we ride on." Then he turned and began to look carefully at the plants which bloomed everywhere in that place. From time to time, Gawain leaned down to examine one more closely, or to pick a few leaves and sniff their fragrance. At last he seemed to find the one he wanted, and carefully picked a few leafy stalks.

"Oh," cried Maudisante, "this is past bearing! That I should stoop to riding with a kitchen boy who cannot resist gathering herbs for the pot!"

"It is not as you think, my lady," said Gawain. "As I rode through the woods, a short way from here, I found a wounded knight, lying as if dead under a great oak tree. If I can find him again, this herb may cure him and restore him to health."

"That's certainly a step up," said the lady disdainfully. "The kitchen boy turned physician! Now all you need to do is to learn to sell jars of ointment, and your fortune will be made." But she turned her horse and followed Gawain as he rode back toward the glade where he had left the knight lying.

The knight was still there, and still seemed to be just barely alive. Sir Gawain dismounted, and gently rubbed the ailing knight with the fragrant herb, placing a few of its leaves under his tongue. Presently the knight stirred, sighed, and opened his eyes. It was not long before he was able to speak, and Gawain asked him how he felt.

"Sir knight," said the sick man, "I am alive, and shall soon be better, thanks to you. Now if you will help me to my feet, perhaps my horse can bear me to lodgings where I can rest and recover."

Sir Gawain glanced at the shivering horse, which seemed to droop more than ever. "I fear he is not good for much," he said, "but if you go gently, and do not try to urge him to make haste, I trust he will bear you safely enough."

He helped his companion to rise and left him leaning against the trunk of the tree, while he stepped over to fetch him the miserable, feeble horse. But Gawain had no sooner turned his back than the other knight suddenly jumped forward, with no sign of weakness at all, and grasped the bridle of Gawain's own horse, Gringolet; mounted, and rode off—without so much as a backward glance, leaving the man who had helped him standing there holding the bridle of an all-but-useless horse, which looked as if it would fall down at once under the weight of so big a man as Sir Gawain.

Now the damsel Maudisante laughed and laughed, as if she had never heard of so wonderful a joke. "Kitchen boy," she said, "your station in life seems to be changing continually. Now that you have tried medicine, you are going to have to turn yourself into a page, walking by my side on foot, for that nag will surely not carry you far."

Gawain turned to inspect the horse more carefully. Indeed, it did seem that the damsel was right. He adjusted its girth, and considered whether there might be some use he could put it to.

"Tell me," said Maudisante, "are you a horse doctor, too? So versatile a man shall surely never lack bread! But come now, it is time to end this silly game—you cannot mean to go on like this."

"Whether I walk or ride, I shall continue to be at your service," Sir Gawain replied. He then tied his shield and spear to the horse's back—which was about as much of a burden as it could carry—and calmly made ready to depart.

"Ah," she said, "I see that you are preparing to go into trade, and are loading your wares on that horse. Take care, lest the customs men levy a great tax on your valuable merchandise!"

But Gawain paid no attention to her gibes, and asked her courteously which road they should now take to find the Castle of Ladies. And so they went on, a rather strange pair of companions: the lady, dressed in fine silks and riding a splendid Arabian horse, while behind her, on foot in the dusty roadway, walked the knight, whose armor looked less and less bright, leading a feeble horse which carried a shield and spear.

Crossing the Last River

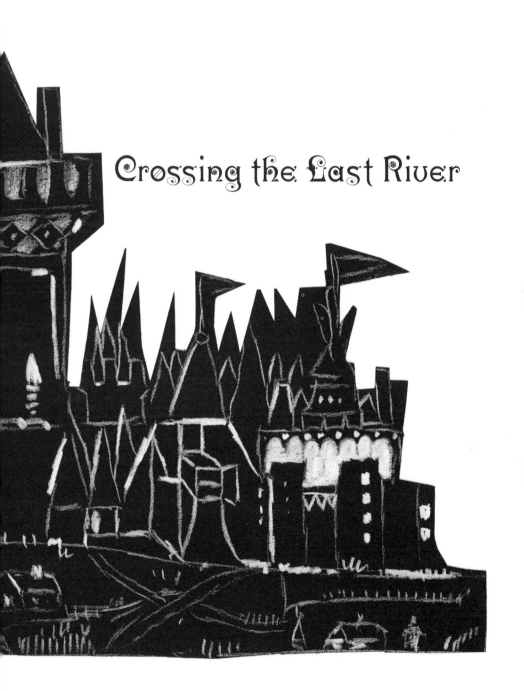

audisante led Gawain along a narrow, winding road, until the land curved down toward a broad, open meadow bordered by bluffs dropping to a rocky beach. This was the bank of a great river, so broad that one could not be sure whether the land beyond might not be an island in the sea. Whatever it was, on it stood a vast and splendid castle with so many towers that Sir Gawain could not begin to count them.

The lady now pulled up her horse and gestured across the water. "That," she said, "is the Castle of Ladies. But if its mistress is preparing a welcome for you, you are not likely to find it to your taste. That is, if you could reach it—which you cannot, unless you can turn yourself into a fish."

"There must be a ferry," Gawain said, looking at the pier at the edge of the water.

"Perhaps; but the ferryman's duty is to bring provisions out to the castle, not to welcome intruders. But maybe you intend to offer your services as a scullion in the castle kitchens? No doubt there are plenty of pans to be scrubbed and spits to be turned, and you, of course, are an expert in these arts. I would not wish to keep you from returning to your proper place!"

But as she spoke, Sir Gawain heard the sound of a horse approaching, and he turned to see what this might mean. Across the field, an armed knight was charging toward him: the way in which he held his shield and spear left no question that he was about to attack.

"Aha!" cried the damsel Maudisante. "Here comes one who will soon teach you that you were never meant to be a knight!" And with that, she turned her horse and fled off into the forest.

Sir Gawain could see that the hostile knight had no intention of dismounting, and, rather than be ridden down on the spot, he grasped his shield and spear and leapt on to the horse he had been leading. The horse did not fall to the ground, but neither was he willing to take a step forward. He stood trembling, as if rooted to the place, as the other came thundering down. Gawain raised his spear, and his foe no sooner came crashing into him than both men were knocked off their horses to the ground.

Gawain was the first to jump up, with his sword ready in his hand. On foot, the battle was no longer unfairly swayed by the quality of the horses, but Sir Gawain found the strange knight still a dangerous opponent, who fought fiercely and recklessly. At last, however, he was a little too reckless, and Gawain was able to catch him off-guard and overpower him. He lay helpless in the dust, while Sir Gawain unlaced his helmet. Only then did Gawain notice, to his great surprise, that this was the ungrateful knight whom he had so recently tended in his deathlike swoon.

"Sir knight," said Gawain in a stern voice, "you have ill repaid me for my kindness to you. Surrender to me at once, or you shall not be so fortunate again."

"I will never surrender," gasped the other, raising his clenched fist. "I would rather die than yield myself a prisoner to any man."

"You are talking great nonsense," said Gawain. "Get up and give me your oath that you will not try to escape."

But the other refused and continued to beg for death. At length, Gawain pulled the reins from the feeble and worthless horse, and bound his prisoner hand and foot, leaving him lying there. Then he sat down himself on the grass to rest, wondering what to do with this awkward package. He looked around for Maudisante, but she had disappeared and was nowhere to be seen.

Now Gawain considered the horse that the defeated knight had been riding when he attacked. It was well armored for battle, and covered with silken hangings—so well covered that nothing of the horse itself was visible except the eyes, the tips of the ears, and the hoofs. Yet it was easy to see that it was a fine, powerful steed. Gawain decided to try it out, and mounted into the saddle, whereupon the horse took off in a series of joyous leaps. "Ah, is that you, Gringolet?" said Sir Gawain, delighted to find his old companion. "Who has put such armor on you, since I saw you last?"

He quickly dismounted again, and patted Gringolet's nose—for it was indeed his own horse. Gringolet whinnied in greeting.

Now a ferryman approached from the pier, where he had left a boat tied at the landing. He had been hunting birds along the river, and carried a gray sparrow hawk perched on his wrist. "God save you, noble sir," he said to Sir Gawain. "I have watched your fight from a distance, and see that you have overcome the other; but I believe it is his horse you are leading there. It is the custom in this place that the loser of a battle forfeits his horse to me. The horse you lead is thus my due, and you should yield it to me, like an honorable knight."

Alas, thought Sir Gawain, *am I to lose my horse so soon when I have just won him back?* He cast about in his mind to find some way out of the predicament. To gain time, he asked, "But what would you do with him, ferryman? You do not need a horse in your boat on the river."

"Of course not," said the ferryman agreeably. "But I can sell him for a great deal of gold, which will help to support my family for many days."

"Then," answered Sir Gawain, "I will give you something better, if you will let me keep my horse—he is really mine, for this base fellow stole him from me. His own horse, to be sure, would be of small value to you, for it is all but useless; but if I give you the prisoner himself, no doubt he will be worth a considerable ransom. That way you will stand to gain much more than by selling any horse."

The ferryman gladly agreed; as for the prisoner himself, no one cared what he had to say about it. "But, sir," said the ferryman, "I do not think I can handle so great a prize by myself. Will you help me to get him into my boat?"

"Willingly," said Gawain, "and I will do more than that: I will unload him from the boat at your very door."

"Then you will be well received there," the ferryman replied. "Dear sir, do me the honor to stay at my house yourself tonight. It will be a great joy for me and my family to entertain so noble a guest, one who has made us so splendid a gift. The sun is growing low in the sky, and you must be weary after your day's ride and the battle here."

Gawain was happy to accept his offer, so he carried the bound prisoner into the boat, while the ferryman led the two horses. The boatman pushed off; they floated for a short distance along the bank of the river, until they pulled it to shore again by a pleasant stone cottage where several children ran out to greet their father. To the eldest, a flaxen-haired girl, the ferryman said, "Take my honored guest, and see that he is made comfortable; we have much to thank him for."

The other, less willing guest he put in charge of two of his sons, warning them to guard him well. To a third, he gave the horses, to be led to the stables for the night—ill-matched pair that they were! Meanwhile, his daughter, a charming maiden not quite thirteen years old, led Gawain to a pleasant chamber. Rushes covered the floor, with gay flowers strewn on top of them. The maiden fetched soft pillows, and arranged them along one wall, spreading a quilt over them to make a couch for the noble guest, while one of her younger brothers spread out a tablecloth and brought bread and water.

Now the host and his wife entered, bearing a platter of roasted quail—the catch from the day's hunting—along with dishes of sauce, and bowls of parsley and lettuce dressed with vinegar. The host urged Gawain to eat, but he would not dine alone and begged them all to join him.

"Bless you, sir," said the housewife, "but I fear that we are not used to the company of gentlemen; my daughter, indeed, is so young she would scarcely know how to behave."

"In any case," said Gawain, "I insist that she sit by my side and share my meal with me."

Blushing, the timid maiden sat down beside him, and cut the meat on his plate, laying the morsels on the slices of bread, which he passed to the others. Only then, when all had been served, would Gawain eat his own share of the meal, though there was little enough to feed so many mouths.

When every speck of the food had disappeared, the family cleared away the cloth and prepared to retire for the night. But first, the host asked Sir Gawain whether there was anything else they could do for him. "Indeed there is," Gawain replied. "Tomorrow, in the morning, I must go on to the castle across the river. Will you ferry me over?"

"Ask me anything else but that, for the love of God," said the host, turning pale. "You are asking me to take you to your death, which would be a terrible return for the favor you have done for us."

"Nevertheless, that is what I ask," said Sir Gawain calmly.

"Oh, no, sir," cried the young maiden, quite forgetting her bashfulness in her distress. "That is the Castle of Ladies, and no man has ever come out of it alive."

"The child is right," said her father. "Pray forget that dangerous idea; I myself would not dream of getting out of my boat on the other side of the water, though I cross it often enough. We call this river the Last River, for whoever sets foot on the land beyond it will never cross another."

"Yet that is where I must go," insisted the knight.

At last they saw that he was firm in his resolve, and that they could not dissuade him from the venture. The ferryman finally agreed that he would bear him over the water in the morning. But there were tears in every eye when the family bade him good night.

In the morning, as they pushed out to cross the river, the housewife and her children stood silently on the bank, grief written on their kindly faces. They clearly did not think to see their noble guest again.

The Perilous Bed

eluctantly the ferryman drew the boat closer and closer to the opposite shore. As they drew nearer to the castle, Sir Gawain gazed at it eagerly. There seemed to be crowds of people on the ramparts and in every window, watching the boat approach. As they drew nearer still, Sir Gawain could see that all of those who thronged there were ladies. Their veils and dresses fluttered in the wind like so many gay banners. "Tell me, good ferryman," said Gawain, "are there no men in this castle?"

"Nay, sir," said the boatman. "None but ladies have ever seen the inside of those walls."

"But who built them then?" Gawain asked. "And who protects all those ladies from oppressors?"

"They need no protection," the ferryman said grimly. "Nor was any man's skill needed to pile the stone for the castle, or fashion its high towers. She who is mistress of the castle can do anything she pleases—it is best not to ask how."

"She is a very powerful lady then?"

"None more powerful" was the reply.

"Then," asked Gawain, "why does she choose to live so far away from others? And why—"

But the ferryman held up his hand to stop the questions. "I can tell you no more of the Castle of Ladies," he said, "save that it is as dangerous as it is beautiful; and so, they say, is its mistress, the Lady of Many Faces, whose name it is forbidden for me to speak."

Gawain could see that his kindly host was pale and tense, and he held his tongue and did not bother him further. At last the boat slipped into a mooring under the castle wall. "This is as far as I can go," said the ferryman. "I shall pray to God to shield you, and have mercy on you."

"I leave my good horse, Gringolet, in your care," said Sir Gawain, "until I return."

The ferryman's reply was so low he could hardly hear it, but it sounded like "If you return—." He looked away, into the water, and would not even turn his eyes to watch as Sir Gawain leapt off onto the shore and turned toward the castle gate—which stood wide open.

Now Gawain went on through the gate and found himself in a great courtyard, as big as the field in which he had lately jousted in the tournament at Tintagel. Ramparts running from tower to tower rose up from it on every side, but only one of the many doorways leading inside the walls stood open. That was the tall gateway which led into the central hall. As Sir Gawain turned to that entrance, he saw that the roof over the hall was the color of peacock feathers, gleaming blue and green in the sun; never before had he seen so beautiful a roof.

But as he entered the hall, he saw that such a roof was only fitting, for everything inside the castle appeared to be of a splendor that Arthur himself might well have envied. Even the window frames were fluted, and over each window rose a delicate canopy carved out of stone, but looking more like fine lace, which carried one's eyes up to the vaulted ceiling where every rib was richly carved and gilded. The floor was strewn with carpets of bright colors, and on the walls hung shimmering tapestries. But nowhere were there couches or seats of any kind.

Sir Gawain could hear footsteps, and the sound of voices not too far away, but there was no one at all in the courtyard or the huge room where he stood. So he began to look for a way into the other parts of the castle. He found a great many doorways, each one fitted with a huge door carved with animals, leaves, and all

49

sorts of designs; but every one of the doors seemed to be bolted fast from the other side. Gawain saw that he would have to wait until someone chose to appear.

But no one came, though the day wore on, and he continued to hear sounds of life all around him. He went out into the courtyard again, and cried out loudly; the only result was a sudden hush, but that did not last long. The sounds as of people whispering in nearby rooms around him resumed as before. He tried to pry open some of the doors with his spear, but it did him no good. There was nothing at all he could do except to wait and see what might happen.

Gawain spent a long afternoon and evening looking at the tapestries and the carvings around the room. Most of them seemed to show forests full of strange wild birds, beasts, and serpents. Gawain saw there a pelican and a phoenix, a unicorn and a manticore, a griffin and a basilisk, as well as many dragons, worked among bright flowers and leafy tendrils. When he had seen everything there was to be seen in the room, he stared out the windows, but the surrounding walls cut off the view. He walked around restlessly, turning about the courtyard, until night fell and it grew dark. Inside the great hall, there was no comfortable place to rest; Sir Gawain had to spend the first part of the night alternately pacing around the room and perching on the window ledges.

Midnight came, and suddenly a bell rang out. Gawain turned in the direction from which the sound came, and saw that one of the doors had swung open. Walking quickly to the doorway, he saw a room with a remarkable paved floor. The pavement seemed to be made of precious stones, and it was as shiny and smooth as glass. It was very difficult to walk on it, for Gawain found that his feet seemed to slip out from under him as he tried to step into the room.

Otherwise, the room was much like the outer hall, except that it was smaller and it contained a bed. This was a very strange-looking bed indeed: it had no canopy, nor any of the other hangings one would expect in a well-appointed castle, and the bed posts did not rest directly on the floor but were attached to wheels, on which the bed seemed to be sliding continuously around the room.

Restless as it was, Gawain determined to try his luck with the bed. He was not so rash as to undress for the night, but kept on every bit of his armor, with his sword and shield firm in his hands. Thus he made his way up to the rolling bed. But it would not hold still long enough for him to climb into it. Every time he reached for it, it flew off halfway across the room. Trying to catch it, he skidded and fell onto the floor once or twice, until he finally decided that the only thing to do was to stand absolutely still until the bed came back in his direction. When it did, and was almost about to run him down, he sprang into it with one great leap.

51

No sooner did Sir Gawain lie down in the bed than it began to move even more violently than it had before. Now it speeded around the room, bumping into one wall or another with a terrible crash every few minutes. There was not much chance of going to sleep with this sort of thing going on. But Gawain lay still, holding on to the posts so that he would not be thrown out, and let the bed clatter about. At last it stopped, with a final jolt, right in the center of the room; the knight found the sudden quiet even more terrible than what had been happening before, since he suspected that some new tricks were about to start. But still he did not budge, except to draw his shield over him carefully.

A few minutes later, he had good reason to be thankful for that stout shield, as well as for his helmet and other armor. Suddenly a shower of stones hailed down on him, pelting him as if the ceiling were raining rocks. Some of them dented his shield badly, while others bruised his legs through the chain mail; but he lay quietly and endured it. When that stopped, it was only to be followed by a cloud of sharp arrows flying from every corner of the room. Again there was nothing he could do but protect himself as best he could with his shield. It was clear that he was not likely to get a good night's sleep in the perilous bed.

At last, the whine of the arrows stopped, and it was quiet again. Sir Gawain ventured to sit up, and swept the arrow shafts from his shield with his sword. Some were sticking into his chain mail, and he pulled them out and brushed off the stones from the bed. As he did so, his hand lighted on a larger object: it was the golden ball little Obilot had given him, which he had been carrying tucked in a fold of his garments.

Just then he heard a very peculiar noise; rather like a chorus of shrill flutes, but there was nothing sweet or musical about this noise. Gawain looked at the door through which the sound seemed to be coming, one hand upon the hilt of his sword. In a few moments, the door burst open, and in stalked a hideous beast like no other creature on earth. Its body resembled that of a lion, but its tail seemed to end in a great barb, and its face would have terrified any but the bravest of men. It had blood-red eyes, glowing like coals of fire, and seemed to have an extra row of tusklike teeth, as it opened its horrible mouth with a high-pitched snarl.

Gawain had never seen such a monster before, but he knew all too well what it was: a manticore, the most bloodthirsty of man-eating beasts, with a poisonous sting in its tail. It was now gathering itself to spring, and Sir Gawain knew that in a moment it would fly at him. As it began to leap, Gawain threw the golden ball, which was still in his hand, so that it went straight into the manticore's mouth and lodged in its throat.

The manticore fell back slightly, choking, as Sir Gawain leapt out of the bed and rushed upon it with his sword. He did not escape the claws and stinging tail of the furious beast, but he was able to drive his blade to the hilt in the manticore's heart before the beast could rid itself of the ball in its throat and turn to rend the knight with its terrible teeth. The manticore fell, quite lifeless; Gawain found himself slipping in the blood that streamed on the already slippery floor.

Weakened by all the blows he had already endured, and in terrible pain from the sting of the manticore's tail, Sir Gawain grew dizzy, and sank down onto the floor next to its body. There, exhausted, he fell into a deep swoon, with his head pillowed on the flank of the dead beast.

The Sword of the Strange Scabbard

hen Sir Gawain came to his senses and opened his eyes, he found three ladies kneeling beside him. One of them was removing his helmet, and one held a basin of water, while the third was gently wiping his face with a damp cloth. He struggled to sit up when he saw them, but the lady who was tending to his face pushed him back, saying, "Nay, sir, do not attempt to rise yet. You have been badly hurt. You must let us remove your armor and treat your wounds."

"Are there no more enemies to fight?" asked the wounded knight. "If there are, I beg you to let me up."

"There are no enemies here now," said the lady in a gentle voice. "You have earned the freedom of the castle. But you must not try to speak any more right now. I am going to give you something that will make you sleep; when you wake up, you will feel much better."

With these words, she put a sprig of herb into Gawain's mouth, and at once he began to feel drowsy. As he drifted off to sleep, he was dimly aware that the ladies were pulling off his coat of mail and rubbing ointment on his wounds and bruises.

Some hours later, he awoke and found he had been carried into another room, where he lay in a comfortable bed quite unlike the one in which he had lain the night before. Several smiling maidens stood at hand to offer him food and fresh water to drink. But they would not let him get up, though he felt ashamed to lie at his ease with ladies standing up around him. One of them stepped to his bedside and said, "It is evening—you may see that the candles are burning. It will be time enough for you to rise in the morning."

After they had seen that he had everything that might make him comfortable, they left him alone. He thought he could not possibly sleep any more, but soon he was fast asleep again, and slumbered until the morning light came through the window. Now he woke up feeling in perfect health and was surprised to find, as he stirred and sat up in his bed, that all his bruises and wounds had disappeared completely, as if the stones and arrows and the manticore itself had all been part of a bad dream. But his shirt, which was lying near the bed, was stained with blood, so it was clear that he had not dreamed the battle.

Fresh, new clothes were also lying there, and he dressed himself in these. His armor had been cleaned and lay in a tidy heap, but there seemed to be no reason to put it on as yet. Thus, dressed in fine silk garments, he went to the door of his chamber, which opened easily, and stepped out to explore the castle for the first time. No one else seemed to be stirring as yet, except for some sounds from the courtyard, where, he saw, a group of maidens were drawing water from a well.

Gawain began to explore. He found many fine rooms, with much to admire, and windows looking out on beautiful gardens. At last he came upon a winding staircase leading up to the highest tower of the castle, and he climbed up, turn after turn of the stairs, until he reached a room at the very top. This room seemed to be very plain; unlike the other rooms of the castle, it had no decorations at all. Walls and floors were of plain rough stone, and the ceiling was simply timbered. There was nothing remarkable about it at all, except for a shining pillar which stood in the center of the circular room.

The pillar was of polished metal, which looked like silver or burnished steel, and it reflected scenes and images like a mirror. But the odd thing was that Sir Gawain could not see what it was reflecting. As he looked into the pillar, he thought he saw a forest of trees, with the leaves rustling in the breeze; but there were no trees in that room, nor were any close enough to be seen through the windows. When he looked back at the pillar again, this time he thought he could see the waves of the ocean, with a ship coming into view; but there were no sails to be seen through the windows of the tower, nor even a ripple on the calm surface of the water before the castle.

Gawain was sorely puzzled. The only thing that was clear to him was that this was indeed a very strange castle, full of wonders, and it was not surprising that people were afraid to enter it. He sat down on the window ledge to watch the changing scenes in the shining pillar.

He jumped up at once when a lady appeared in the doorway. She was one of the three who had knelt by his side after his fight with the manticore—the one who had given him the herb to make him sleep. She was tall and queenly, and richly dressed; she was very beautiful, but there was nothing soft about her, and it would have been hard to say how old she might have been. There was something about the expression of her eyes that was as old as time.

"Good morning, Gawain," said the lady. "Did you not recognize me?"

"No, lady," said Sir Gawain. Somehow, he was not at all surprised that she knew *his* name.

She smiled. "I am your aunt," she said, "Morgan, whom men call Morgan le Fay. The others who were with me last night were my two sisters: your other aunt, Morcades, and your own mother, Morgause."

"What," said Sir Gawain, "is my mother here? I must go and greet her."

"Not yet," answered Morgan le Fay. "There will be time

enough. First, I want you to tell me what brought you to my castle. Surely you knew that we have never allowed a man within these walls before? Those few who have dared to try to gain entrance have been—stopped."

"I had heard that," said Sir Gawain. "But my need was great. Only with your help can I rescue a lady in sore distress." And he told her about how Sir Kay had failed on his quest to save the lady of Montesclaire, and of how he himself had learned that the Sword of the Strange Scabbard was within the Castle of Ladies.

When he had told his whole story, Morgan moved to the center of the room, and stretched out a hand to him. "Come," she said, "let us look into this pillar. Then perhaps we can see more clearly what is to be done."

Then they gazed into the pillar, and soon the figure of Maudisante, the lady of Logres, appeared, riding through a wood. She seemed to be searching for something. Gawain exclaimed with surprise as he recognized her, but Morgan le Fay simply nodded, as if that were what she had expected to see. "Perhaps she is looking for me," said Gawain.

"Perhaps, but it may be for someone or something else. The pillar will tell us," said Morgan. And soon the scene changed. They saw a captive knight, pacing somewhat restlessly around a simple room.

"That," said Sir Gawain, "is the knight who so ungratefully took my horse, whom I overcame in the field at the side of the river. He is a prisoner in the house of the ferryman."

"His name is Uriance," said Morgan le Fay. "He is the man for whom the lady Maudisante searches."

Now that scene faded from the pillar, too, and in its place appeared a forbidding tower, surrounded by a spiky stockade. It

59

appeared to have only the smallest of windows—little more than slits—and very few of those.

"That looks like a dungeon," said Sir Gawain.

"I expect that it is just that," said Morgan le Fay. "It is probably the dungeon where the lady of Montesclaire is imprisoned. Did you say she was guarded by a terrible beast?"

"That is what I have been told," Gawain replied, and he peered closely to see what he could see of the creature that guarded the dungeon. But Morgan le Fay drew him back.

"I would not look too closely," she said. "I am not sure it is safe, even in the image of the pillar, for that is a basilisk: its glance can turn a man to stone."

Gawain obeyed. He had heard of the basilisk's glance. He knew, too, that the breath of a basilisk was poisonous in itself and could drive a man mad.

Morgan added, "It seems likely that the strange state in which you saw Sir Kay, as well as that from which you saved Sir Uriance, was caused by the basilisk. No man would have a chance of getting past such a guardian—unless, perhaps, he could make use of the Sword of the Strange Scabbard. I see that I must let you take it."

Now she turned, and led him to a small cupboard in the wall, so well hidden that he had not realized it was there. From this she took a sword, sheathed in a scabbard, which she held in her hands.

Sir Gawain stared at it, finding it difficult to believe that this was the sword he was looking for. "But I do not see anything strange about that scabbard," he said. "It looks very plain—a very ordinary scabbard."

Morgan le Fay smiled slowly. "It is not the way it looks that has won it its name," she said. "Without this scabbard, the sword would be of little use to anyone. And it is no ordinary sword. Stand back from me a space, and I will show you its nature."

Gawain retreated a few paces. Then Morgan slowly drew the sword from its scabbard. As soon as she started to pull at the hilt, a wonderful, sweet odor of roses and precious spices seemed to fill the room; and then, as the sword itself began to appear, wild strains of music were heard, and suddenly Gawain was faint and sleepy. He rubbed his eyes, but felt he simply could not stay awake. Just as he was about to crumple to the floor, fast asleep, Morgan put the sword back in its scabbard. At once the music stopped, though the sweet fragrance seemed to linger in the air, and Gawain was wide awake again.

"The battle song of this sword," explained Morgan le Fay, "will

put any enemy to sleep. Only the man who holds it can stay awake when it sings. But its power comes from the scabbard in which it rests, which constantly renews the spell; without the Strange Scabbard, this sword would soon become like any other. If you wish to conquer a basilisk, you must start to draw the sword from its scabbard as soon as you think you are coming close to the monster. Then it will be asleep by the time you come upon it, and its glance cannot harm you. Further, the scent which comes from the scabbard will cover the odor of the basilisk's breath, and protect you from its poison. But you must work quickly, to slay the monster before the effect begins to wear off.''

Now she handed the sword to Sir Gawain, who received it as the great treasure it was. "But tell me, good aunt," he said, "how I am to find the prison of the lady of Montesclaire? Her sister never told me where it was, and now I do not even know how to find Maudisante herself.''

"Ever since you began this quest," said Morgan le Fay, "you have had help and guidance from one lady after another. I do not doubt that one will appear at the right moment to lead you on from here.''

Now she did not wish to discuss the matter any further, and suggested that it was time for Sir Gawain to go down to see his mother and his other aunt, Morcades. Gawain was glad to do this. But his quest was not out of his mind for a moment. Nor did the three ladies wish to keep him, when the other two had heard the story; and so Sir Gawain was soon ready to cross the river again, and start on what he hoped would be the last stage of his journey.

Sir Gawain's Quest

horn was sounded, as a signal to the ferryman, while Sir Gawain made his farewells to the three queens and the other ladies of their castle. Thus, when he went out the gate and arrived at the landing, his friend was already there at the pier. The good boatman was overjoyed to see Gawain, and wept with relief as he embraced him. The trip back across the river was a good deal more cheerful than the trip over had been!

When the boat reached shore, the ferryman's family came running to give Gawain a joyous welcome. The boys rushed to fetch Gringolet, for Sir Gawain explained that he could not possibly stay with them now; he must continue on his quest, if there were to be any chance of success. "Even so," he added, "it is going to be very difficult, for I do not know just where I should go. If only I knew how to find the damsel Maudisante, I would be well on the way."

Now the ferryman's daughter spoke. "Sir," she said, "if you wish to find the lady of Logres, I think I can guide you to her."

Rejoicing, Gawain said, "Fair maiden, I should have known that you could; I was told that a lady would guide me when I had need."

Blushing, the young girl replied, "I do not think I am worthy of that title, but I will gladly do what I can for you."

Sir Gawain assured her that she was as fair and courteous as any lady in the land. He promised her anxious parents that he would see that she returned home safely as soon as possible, and rode off with his young guide perched before him on the saddle.

The maiden led him along the banks of the river, through meadows and groves of trees, until they came to a pretty little chapel that stood in a clearing by itself. "I think, sir," said she,

"that you will find the lady Maudisante here. She often comes to pray at the tomb of her father, which is in this place, and I saw her ride by this way only this morning."

Sir Gawain dismounted and entered the chapel. There on one side the damsel Maudisante was kneeling. Gawain stood very still for a moment, watching her; he thought that she was more beautiful than any of the lovely ladies in the Castle of Ladies, and was a bit surprised to find that he had missed her, despite her sharp tongue.

In a few minutes, Maudisante became aware of Gawain's presence. She rose at once, and went outside with him, gazing at him with an eager expression he had never before seen on her face. "Ah, sir knight," she said—and Sir Gawain did not fail to note that it was the first time she had addressed him as anything but a kitchen boy—"where have you been these last two days? I could not find a trace of either you or Sir Uriance."

"Then you knew who Sir Uriance was?" asked Gawain, astonished.

"Ah, yes," said Maudisante with a sigh. "He is my sister's sweetheart. The sad state in which you found him was the result of an attempt to free his lady. When he took your good horse, and challenged you to battle, he must have been suffering from the mad rashness that seems to overcome all who go anywhere near the awful creature who guards my sister. Alas, that he was so reckless as to try to rescue her without the only weapon that might have prevailed! But where is he now? And which of you conquered the other in battle?'

"Do not be troubled, lady," said Gawain, "for he is safe, though I overcame him. I made him my prisoner, though he was most unwilling, and left him in the care of the ferryman's family, in order that they might receive his ransom. This damsel with me is the ferryman's daughter; she will tell you how he fares."

The maiden assured Maudisante that their prisoner was well, whereupon the lady rejoiced and said that she would see that the ransom was duly paid. But now she again asked Sir Gawain where he had been, and the knight replied, "I have been over the Last River, and have brought back the Sword of the Strange Scabbard."

The lady of Logres was astounded. "Sir knight," she said at last, "I have surely done you a grave injustice. To think that I called you

an unworthy kitchen boy! You have done what all thought could not be done."

Humbly, she asked him his name. When she learned that he was Sir Gawain, she rejoiced greatly. "Now," she said, "let us go and free Sir Uriance that he may ride with us, for at last there may be hope that his dear lady can be saved."

When they returned to the ferryman's cottage, they found Sir Uriance in a far different frame of mind from that which had led him to act so badly a few days ago. Fear for the safety of his lady was now uppermost in his mind, and he was quite ready to welcome the knight who had saved his life, and might perhaps save hers.

Together, Sir Gawain, Sir Uriance, and the lady Maudisante rode on, until Gawain saw on the horizon the very tower which he had seen in Morgan le Fay's marvelous pillar. It looked just as grim as he remembered it, and for a mile or so about, it was surrounded by a bleak desert where no tree grew, nor even tufts of grass, and no living bird or beast was to be seen. The three companions halted on the edge of the wood, for there was no cover in that wasteland to help them approach nearer without being seen.

Sir Uriance, although he had already had reason enough to fear the guardian of the tower, asked to be allowed to ride out with Gawain, saying, "Perhaps I can distract him while you attack." But Sir Gawain begged him to remain there with Maudisante, under the shelter of a lime tree. "For," he said, "if I should fail, it will not help to have you stricken, too."

As Gawain rode out from the wood, he drew the sword that Morgan le Fay had given him from its scabbard, and at once he was surrounded with the wonderful perfume of roses and spices, as the sword sang its wild battle song. He spurred Gringolet and raced across the plain, in order not to waste precious time, until he came upon a sleeping beast just outside the spikes which surrounded the tower. For a moment he caught his breath in surprise, for it did not really look as dangerous as one might have thought; it was actually quite small, and did not seem particularly frightening.

But it was a basilisk, without any doubt. It looked rather like a cross between a snake and a chicken, and had white stripes running the length of its body. Gawain knew he had better not pause to look at it for any length of time, for already the singing of the sword was beginning to grow a little fainter, and if it should fade away the creature would be wide awake again. Quickly he struck off the basilisk's head, and the danger was past.

70

When they saw that blow, Uriance and Maudisante rode rejoicing from the shelter of the tree, and all three now passed through the open gate of the tower; with such a fearful guardian outside, the enchanter who had placed it there had seen no need for further protection.

They searched for the lady of Montesclaire, calling her name over and over, until at last a faint voice answered from a room high up in the tower. There they found her lying on the bare floor, half-dead from hunger and thirst. By keeping her on a diet of bread and water, and little enough of either, the wicked enchanter had thought to make her so weak that she would do whatever he wanted her to do; but the lady had somehow endured, and her joy, weak as she was, was touching to behold when she saw her rescuers.

Gently they carried her down the stairs, and out into the air, where Sir Uriance placed her before him on his horse—the very same horse that had seemed so useless before. But that was the basilisk's doing, too, and the horse, like the master, had now recovered from the evil effects.

Thus they rode back to Maudisante's castle of Logres, where she ordered her servants to do everything necessary to care for her weakened sister. Sir Gawain's quest might have been thought to be over. But it was not quite, for he had in mind to win one final prize to bring back with him to Camelot. It was not until the damsel Maudisante had agreed to go to the court of King Arthur as Sir Gawain's own lady that Gawain's personal quest ended just as he had wished.

Thus it happened that when Sir Gawain was ready to return to Camelot, he did not ride alone, but with the lady of Logres, and her sister, the lady of Montesclaire, and Sir Uriance. Nor did he forget that he had another, much younger, lady. When they reached

Tintagel, he found his friend Obilot and told her of all his adventures, and of how important her ball had been in a moment of need.

"Now," he said, "perhaps you may ride with me after all, if you will come to court to be a bridesmaid at my wedding."

Obilot was delighted, and the count and countess had no objection. So Obilot went to Camelot, too, where a great wedding feast was held. All Sir Gawain's friends were invited, from kings and queens to the ferryman and his family. The lord of Cavalon was there, with his sister, Belacuel, and Gawain offered to return the Sword of the Strange Scabbard to them. But they gave it as a wedding present to the knight who had used it so well.

Not even Morgan le Fay could send a gift that Sir Gawain treasured more.

About the Author

As a medieval scholar, Constance Hieatt has especially enjoyed retelling Arthurian legends for young readers. THE CASTLE OF LADIES is a companion volume to her earlier books: *Sir Gawain and the Green Knight, The Knight of the Lion, The Knight of the Cart, The Joy of the Court,* and *The Sword and the Grail.* Mrs. Hieatt is a specialist in Old and Middle English, and the author of several texts, translations, and scholarly commentaries. She has taught at Queensborough Community College and at St. John's University in New York, and is now Professor of English at the University of Western Ontario in London, Ontario.

Mrs. Hieatt was born in Boston, Massachusetts, and attended Smith College. She received her A.B. and A.M. degrees from Hunter College, and her Ph.D. from Yale University. She and her husband, who is also a professor of English, spend much of their time in England, where their home is part of a remodeled manor house in a village near Oxford.

About the Artist

Norman Laliberté is perhaps most widely known as the creator of the heraldic banners that adorned the Vatican Pavilion at the 1963 World's Fair in New York.

Born in Worcester, Massachusetts, and brought up in Montreal, Mr. Laliberté was graduated from the Institute of Design in Chicago with a B.A. in visual arts and a M.S. in art education. His work has been exhibited in major museums and galleries throughout the country. He has also written and illustrated books on various aspects of traditional art, and he describes his experience in illustrating THE CASTLE OF LADIES as "like a trip in a faraway place."

L